CUENTO DE LUZ

To Adriel, Marc, and Yuna; for always walking by my side.
— Susanna Isern

To Eva, Vera, and Mario, the "secret" ingredients that fill my day-to-day with flavor, as well as some nights.
To Miguel, Jaime, and Bruno, the guinea pigs of my first recipes.
— Daniel Montero Galán

STONE PAPER®
NO TREES - NO WATER - NO BLEACH

This book is printed on **Stone Paper©** that is Silver **Cradle to Cradle™** certified.

Cradle to Cradle™ is one of the most demanding ecological certification systems, awarded to products that have been conceived and designed in an ecologically intelligent way.

Certified B Corporation®

Cuento de Luz™ became a **Certified B Corporation©** in 2015. The prestigious certification is awarded to companies which use the power of business to solve social and environmental problems and meet higher standards of social and environmental performance, transparency, and accountability.

A Mystery in the Forest
Text © 2020 del texto: Susanna Isern
Illustrations © 2020 de las ilustraciones: Daniel Montero Galán
© 2020 Cuento de Luz SL
Calle Claveles, 10 | Urb. Monteclaro | Pozuelo de Alarcón | 28223 | Madrid | Spain
www.cuentodeluz.com
Original title in Spanish: *Un misterio en el bosque*
English translation by Jon Brokenbrow
ISBN: 978-84-16733-92-7
Printed in PRC by Shanghai Cheng Printing Company February 2020, print number 1806-5

A Mystery
in the
Forest

Susanna Isern

Daniel Montero Galán

Every morning, just as day is breaking, Deer leaves his house, turns left at the fifth pine tree to the right, crosses through the willow wood, wades across the river at its narrowest point, and happily trots into the quietest part of the forest.

Winter is the time for oranges, pears, and apples.

In spring, he gathers strawberries, cherries, and apricots.

Deer is the only one who knows this secret place, where all the best things grow.

In summer, he collects blueberries, raspberries, plums, and figs . . .

And in the autumn, it's time for grapes, chestnuts, walnuts, and hazelnuts.

When his basket is full, he heads home. Then, Deer starts up his wood oven. Sometimes he makes jams; other times he makes fruit in syrup, or dries grapes in the sun while he toasts almonds with sugar.

On special days, he cooks orange cupcakes, walnut cake, cinnamon cookies, or apple pie. An amazing aroma wafts between the houses. All of his neighbors open their doors and windows wide, so the delicious smell can enter their homes.

In the afternoon, Deer sits out in his garden with a cake, a
steaming pot of tea, and a jar of honey. Soon all of the animals
with a sweet tooth who are passing by stop to join him. They
share a snack, laugh, and chat until the sun sets, and the first
crickets begin to chirp.

One morning, as usual, Deer leaves his house early, and heads off to the quietest part of the forest. When he reaches the chestnut tree, he finds a pile of leaves and broken branches.

"Now who would have done that?" he asks himself, more than a little annoyed.

Then he walks over to the grape vines, where the soil has been dug up.

"Has someone been following me?" he thinks, after he sees mysterious paw prints all over the place.

Deer heads back home, puzzled. When he arrives, he discovers something even stranger that makes his hair stand on end. His pots and pans have all been moved, there are crumbs all over the counter, and there is a strong smell of sponge cake. And to make things worse, his beloved Secret Recipe Book has gone missing!

Deer is worried. He goes out to ask his neighbors if they've seen anything strange. But no one has seen anything at all. Suddenly, he spots a suspicious trail of pine nuts heading toward Rabbit's house. Deer follows it at once.

When he arrives, he peers through the window, and sees three little mice rolling around on the kitchen floor. Next to them, there is a horrible-looking cake, covered in bite marks.

"I told you we shouldn't have tried it!" moans one of the mice.

"Rabbit's used us as guinea pigs—well, as guinea mice," says another one.

"Ow, it hurts!" says the third mouse, clutching his tummy.

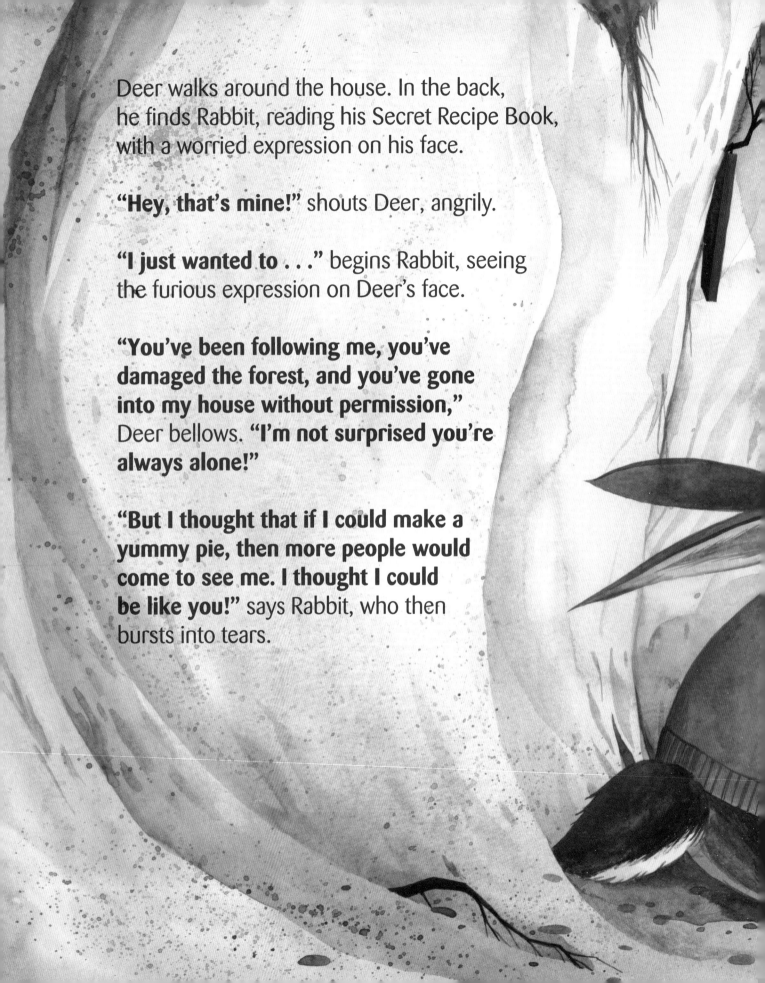

Deer walks around the house. In the back, he finds Rabbit, reading his Secret Recipe Book, with a worried expression on his face.

"Hey, that's mine!" shouts Deer, angrily.

"I just wanted to . . ." begins Rabbit, seeing the furious expression on Deer's face.

"You've been following me, you've damaged the forest, and you've gone into my house without permission," Deer bellows. **"I'm not surprised you're always alone!"**

"But I thought that if I could make a yummy pie, then more people would come to see me. I thought I could be like you!" says Rabbit, who then bursts into tears.

Deer grabs his Secret Recipe Book and storms out, slamming the door as he goes.

"Well, that's all I needed to hear!" he grumbles. But on the way home, Deer reflects on what happened.

That night, Rabbit can't get to sleep. At midnight, he hears a noise.

He nervously climbs out of bed, and peeks out of the window.

By the light of the moon, he can see Deer tiptoeing away in the darkness.

Rabbit walks to the door, opens it, and is surprised to find a mysterious package with his name written on it.

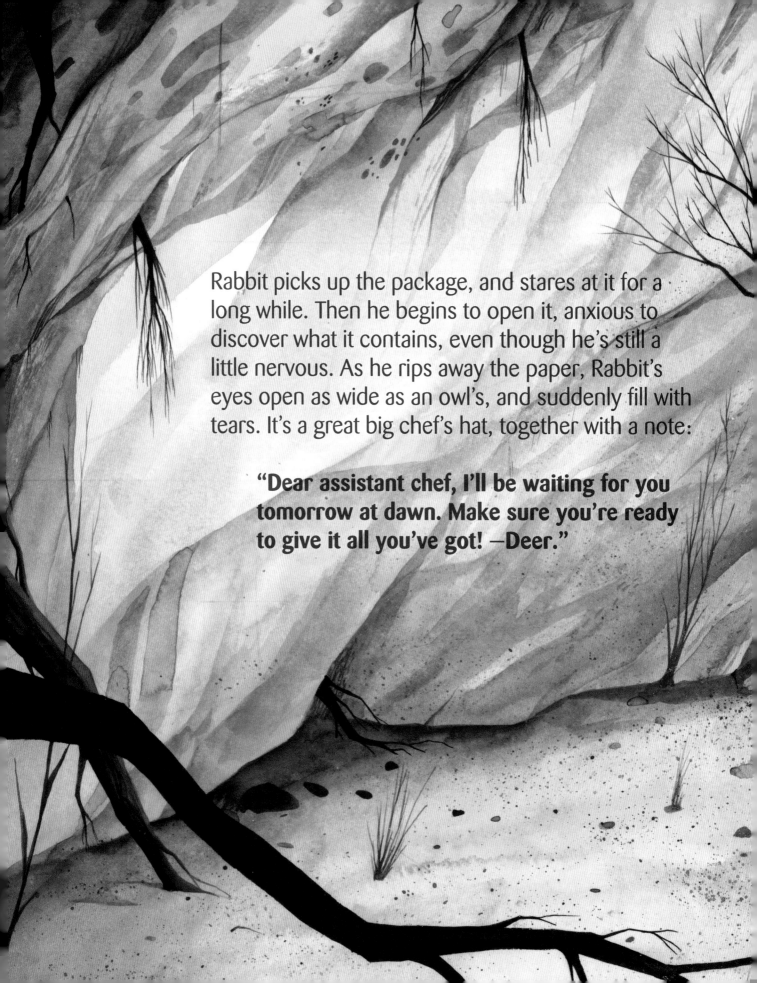

Rabbit picks up the package, and stares at it for a long while. Then he begins to open it, anxious to discover what it contains, even though he's still a little nervous. As he rips away the paper, Rabbit's eyes open as wide as an owl's, and suddenly fill with tears. It's a great big chef's hat, together with a note:

"Dear assistant chef, I'll be waiting for you tomorrow at dawn. Make sure you're ready to give it all you've got! —Deer."

Each morning, Deer and Rabbit now walk together to the fifth pine tree to the right, cross through the willow wood, wade across the river at its narrowest point, and happily trot into the quietest part of the forest.

When they arrive home, they prepare a delicious recipe. In the afternoon, they sit out in the garden with a cake, a steaming pot of tea, and a jar of honey. Soon all of the animals with a sweet tooth who are passing by stop to join them. They share a snack, laugh, and chat until the sun sets, and the first crickets begin to chirp.

Deer's Secret Recipe Book

Apple Pie

Ingredients:
- 4 large eggs
- 1.2 cups of sugar
- 1 small pot of natural yogurt
- 1.7 cups of flour
- 1 sachet of yeast
- 0.7 cups of butter
- A pinch of salt
- Three apples
- Ground cinnamon

Preparation:
Beat the eggs. Keep stirring, and pour in the sugar, the yogurt, the flour and the yeast, the butter, and a pinch of salt.

Chop up one apple and add it to the mixture. After stirring it thoroughly, pour it into a pie tin. Cut the other two apples into thin slices, sprinkle them with cinnamon, and lay them out carefully on top of the dough.

Put the pie tin into an oven that has been preheated to 375 degrees Fahrenheit, and leave it to bake for 45 minutes.

Deer's Secret Ingredient for this recipe:
Smile from sunrise to sunset, and from moonrise to moonset.